last call casanova

A Hope Harbor Romance

karla doyle

When the one woman *not* interested in going home with Anthony is the only one he wants, it's last call for this Casanova...

anthony

I'm back in Hope Harbor, the little town I can't stay away from, for my buddy's wedding to the love of his life. They're perfect together. I'm happy for them, but that kind of relationship isn't in my wheelhouse. Not anymore. Everything changes once there's a picture of you holding an oversized check splashed across the internet. When it's public knowledge you won the lottery and have ten million in the bank, everybody wants a piece of you.

Been there, got burned, and have the scorch marks to prove it. Money's not the only thing I keep locked up now. My heart's in the vault too. But there's one piece of me I've been happy to share since then, and it's guaranteed to satisfy. Looking for a good time? I'm your man. Just don't look for more. That's the rule. Or it was, until I met Mya.

Hope Harbor is full of gorgeous fish happy to hop on my hook anytime I'm in town. Too bad the only one I want doesn't fall for my lines, and has no interest in my pole. Pretty sure she'd be happy if I took a long walk off the end of the short pier and never resurfaced.

The more Mya pushes me away, the more I want to reel her in. The truth is—I'm the one who's hooked. And one night together is all it takes to know I never want to be released.

chapter one

. . .

anthony

WEDDINGS. Women love them because of the fairytale. Men love them because of the women. Dresses, high heels, lowered inhibitions and increased libidos. What's not to love?

Four of my sisters have tied the knot, one of them twice. That's five weddings where I've worn the matched-set rental tux. Add my cousins' weddings and a few old friends' big days to that list, and I've checked the "beef" box on an RSVP card fourteen times.

But I've only checked the "plus one" box once. At this point, I doubt I will again. Casual is easy. Relationships, not so much. Not when you have ten million in the bank and your picture holding the big check has been splashed across the internet. It's easier just to play the part.

Tomorrow's couple don't have to pretend anything. Jensen and Bailey have known each other forever. Loved each other practically as long. All their cards are on the table and they're both winning the game.

I took a turn at that game and lost. People say I'm lucky my ex-fiancée only ripped out my heart, not my bank account. They have no fucking idea how shitty it is to question everything and everyone. To keep your heart under lock and key. But once burned, stay the hell away from the fire. That's survival.

On the subject of "fire," there's a redhead with hot curves directly ahead. Not the woman I'd like to reel in, but my favorite dark-haired bombshell would rather fillet me like a Lake Erie pickerel than let me buy her a drink. Maybe the redhead has more going for her than pretty hair and a nice ass. She might be great—if I don't compare her to Mya.

Time to play the part. Be the carefree player everyone expects. I'm on my way to the bar when tomorrow's bride-to-be bounces into the frame.

"No drinks yet, it's picture time!" Bailey's voice brims with happiness and genuine goodness. That's her natural state, and it seems bigger every time I come to town for a visit. Being madly in love with the man glued to her side agrees with her.

"You know, gorgeous," I say, slinging my arm around her shoulders in front of her fiancé. "The big guy won't be happy when you redecorate your apartment with all these pictures of me."

"Sure I will." Jensen knocks the air out of me when he slaps one of his mountain mitts on my back. "They'll give me something to practice my darts game on."

Beside me, Bailey laughs. She knows Jensen isn't truly jealous and I'm not seriously hitting on her. A complete one-eighty from the first time I met her, a year ago, right here in this bar. The night of Jensen's thirtieth birthday, and his third weekend in business after opening On the Rocks. Bailey walked in looking like a grown man's dream, and I told my university buddy to hook us up. That was the first time Jensen ever refused to be my wingman, and the last time I asked him to be.

Their kind of love is a rare beast. Only an asshole or idiot would try bringing it down. Despite what many people think —what I've let them believe—I'm neither of those things.

"What pictures are we taking this time?" I ask as we approach a table in the corner that's cordoned off with streamers. I'm not camera-shy by any means, but everywhere I turn since arriving in Hope Harbor earlier this week, somebody's waiting to snap another wedding-related picture. Bailey's going to need a lot of photo albums.

"Mya made custom t-shirts for the wedding party. I want us to get a group shot wearing them before everyone scatters."

"Nobody's going to scatter from the best party in town. Except maybe you two," I say when I catch the look passing between them. "Can't wait for the honeymoon?"

"Every night's the honeymoon for them." Mya snorts and shakes her head as we join her and the other wedding-party members at the table. "If you didn't know that, I guess it's true that guys don't talk about personal stuff as much as women."

"Oh, fuck no. I've been subjected to way too many of my sisters' conversations. You women are ruthless with the nitty-gritty sex talk. Men make shit up about people who don't exist or don't matter. We don't share details about our actual sex lives. We don't want other guys knowing that kind of stuff about our women."

"Sounds like you're admitting to lying about all your conquests," Jensen says, sending hoots up from the handful of people in our group.

"Asshole." My friendly jab to his shoulder doesn't move him a fraction of an inch. I'm six-foot-one and no weakling, but my buddy probably has a hundred pounds on me. Maybe more, now that Bailey's cooking for him daily.

"Mya, hand out the shirts," Bailey says, bouncing on the spot. She has a couple of close friends, but Mya is number one. Like most of the people in this town of six thousand, they've known each other since childhood. They're tight like sisters, and just as protective.

I should know. The first time I met Mya was here in this bar, about a month into Bailey and Jensen's relationship. Mya smiled so sweetly, her pretty face could've been made of sugar. The moment Bailey's attention shifted to Jensen, her best friend leaned in and tore me a new one, putting me on notice. She'd been shipping Jensen and Bailey to get together longer than Hope Harbor's been shipping Lake Erie perch. She threatened permanent bodily harm to my favorite appendage if I tried getting between them.

I've had women threaten me before, for much more personal reasons. But there was something about Mya that night. The ferocity and passion in her words and voice. Fuck, in the way she glared at me. I had to laugh in her face just so I didn't kiss her firecracker mouth, right then and there.

For the record—laughing in Mya's face doesn't win any points with her. The opposite. That moment landed me at the top of her shit list, and no amount of charm has changed my status. She's the one woman immune to my charisma.

Initially, I wanted to smooth things over with her for Bailey's sake. Now it's strictly personal. I love spending time with Jensen and Bailey, but Mya is the one who pulls me to Hope Harbor. That "once burned, stay the hell away from the flame" thing? Out the window where she's concerned. I'm the moth to her flame. I can't stay away.

She doesn't know that. She's too busy hating me to find out she might like me. The more we're together—and I make sure that's a lot—the harder she pushes back. As much as I want her to let her walls down and give me a chance, I fucking love her sharp tongue. I'm hooked on all things Mya Martinez.

She passes rolled-up t-shirts to the other groomsman, bridesmaid, then one each to Jensen, Bailey, and me. She keeps one for herself, smiling smugly at me when she snaps hers open. "Hope you all like them."

Our small group becomes a chorus of chatter as the t-shirts are unrolled. Good-natured amusement at the caricatures she created for each person. Kudos for her artistic flair. They're not wrong. She's wickedly talented. A bit wicked too, at least where my drawing is concerned. Her rendition of me is very different from everyone else's, and her opinion of me is in the details. If she'd do this for Bailey's wedding t-shirts, it's safe to say I'm never getting out of her doghouse.

She's still eyeing me when I look up. Waiting for my reaction.

"It's like looking in a mirror." I flash a grin while flipping my t-shirt around for everyone to see.

Laughter erupts in our corner of the bar, drawing the attention of everyone in the bar. I hold up the t-shirt for all to see and receive clapping and laughter in response.

Bailey—sweetheart that she is—issues an, "Oh my God," before staring at Mya. Looks as if the bride didn't see all the t-shirt designs before tonight's unveiling.

"Let's get this party started," I say, unbuttoning my white dress shirt and shrugging it off my shoulders, right there in the bar, under Mya's heated gaze. I pull the t-shirt on, then meet Mya's eyes. "Your turn."

mya

The pre-wedding celebration has been in full swing for over four hours. Bailey and Jensen left ages ago, entrusting Anthony with the festivities. Fair enough, since he's the resident party boy.

Jensen planned to close the bar for the weekend. One less thing to think about during the biggest event of his life. Anthony convinced him to keep On the Rocks open. He *claimed* it was so Jensen wouldn't lose two nights' worth of revenue. He said they might even make more money than a usual Friday night because people would come to see the soon-to-be-married couple the night before their wedding. Then he sweetened the pot by offering to cover staff wages. He called it a wedding gift. Another one. His bank account is the only thing bigger than his ego.

Am I jealous that Anthony can give my friends multiple financially beneficial gifts while I can make them cute t-shirts? Yes. Do I acknowledge that he's not the worst guy in the world? Only to myself. Does he make my blood boil every time we're sharing airspace? God, yes.

Like he's doing *right now*. He hasn't taken off the damn t-shirt since stripping half-naked in front of everyone to put it on. He should've been pissed off at the comic version of him I created. But no, not Anthony. He laughed off my artistic insinuated insults. Then proceeded to spend the rest of the evening looking ridiculously hot in his ridiculous t-shirt.

Brittany Jones certainly doesn't seem to mind Anthony's goofy t-shirt. She's been laughing at everything that's come out of his mouth since he sidled up to her at the bar. Okay, fine, he didn't sidle. He walked right up to her, confidently and directly. As he always does. And why wouldn't he, since it always works. Everything works out for him.

Ugh, I have to stop watching him. Caring who he's with or what he's doing with them. Green is not a good color for me. And I have no reason to be jealous, because there's never been anything between us, aside from the wall I've built. *That* needs to stay solidly in place, because Anthony and I will never be close. Not as friends, and definitely not as more.

Even *if* I lowered my defenses and smiled instead of scowling in his direction, he'd never look at me the way he looks at Brittany, or any of the other women I've watched him flirt with over the past year. Anthony has a type, and I don't fit the mold—I exceed it. In the attitude department and by several dress sizes.

I turn my back on him and tip my beer to my lips. The ice-cold draught slides down my throat, cooling the angry flames he ignites. To hell with him and his great hair, deep laugh, and broad shoulders. I just have to get through this weekend's wedding togetherness, then he'll take his Casanova ways back to Toronto. I'll get a break from the unwelcome feelings he stirs up every time he comes to town.

I reach the bottom of my glass sooner than I'd like. There's no way I'm going to the bar to get a refill. I'm staying as far away from Anthony and Brittany—or whoever he's currently chatting up over there—as possible.

On the Rocks is hopping busy tonight, and I can't catch the attention of the only server in sight as he hustles toward the bar. I'm *not* going over there. I'm not even going to check to see if the coast is clear. There are other ways to get a refill.

I open my phone and fire off a text to the guy filling the drink orders. One of the benefits of living in the small town you grew up in—having the phone number of nearly everyone.

Minutes later, a manly hand slides a fresh draught in front of me.

"That was fast," I say.

"Wouldn't want to keep you waiting."

I pinch my eyes closed at the sound of Anthony's voice. *Shit.* "Thanks." Still avoiding eye contact, I tip my ass to one side and withdraw my credit card from my back pocket. "Did you bring the machine over, or did Lee put it on my tab?"

"Neither. It's on me."

Now I meet Anthony's gaze. "I don't need or want you to buy my drinks."

"Then you'll have to go to the bar next time, instead of texting the bartender. I'm not a guy who'd bring a drink to a beautiful woman and expect her to pay for it."

"I didn't ask you to bring my drink over." That's right, I'm totally ignoring the *beautiful* comment. I know he doesn't mean anything by it.

Anthony flirts the way he breathes—instinctively. Effortlessly. Endlessly.

That angry heat is on the rise again, searing me from my belly to my eyes. "If you won't take my money, I'll go pay at the bar." I rise from my seat, but don't make it half a step.

"Mya, stop," he says, grabbing hold of my upper arms as he blocks my path. "Please."

My eyes widen at that word. At what sounds like honest-to-God sincerity in his voice. Never mind the tingle running through me from his hands on my skin. I refuse to think about that. Damn traitorous, undersexed body.

He exhales, not taking his eyes—or hands—off me. "I generally don't give half a fuck if anybody likes me. But you're not just anybody. You're Bailey's best friend, and a good friend of Jensen's. They're going to be together forever, which means we will be too. It'd be nice if you didn't hate me for the next fifty years."

The thought of spending the rest of my life in constant contact with him initiates a twisty flutter. In my chest. Also, much lower. "I don't hate you. I just—" *Don't want to like you.*

"You didn't trust me not to fuck things up for Bailey and Jensen."

"You couldn't have," I say, because apparently, I'm incapable of exiting the bitch zone when Anthony is in my personal space.

"You're right. But I never would've tried. The night I met Bailey is the night I discovered my best buddy loved her. That made her off-limits. I'm an ass sometimes, but I'm not an asshole. If you got to know me, you'd see there's a difference. Then, maybe you could move the 'I don't hate you' needle closer to 'I like you.'"

Dammit. I hate when the ball's in my court. "Fine."

His dark eyebrows rise at my grumbled huff. "It's that bad, the idea of liking me?"

"Don't push your luck," I say, stabbing his chest with my index finger. "I agreed to *maybe* move the needle. I never promised I'd like you."

"It's a start."

More unwanted tingling ripples through me when he smiles. Because it's not his usual gonna-pick-up-tonight smile, it's warm and genuine, and makes his gray eyes twinkle. Damn him.

I step back enough that his hands slide from my arms, an action that raises goosebumps over my skin. Maybe it's not too late to round up a date for the wedding tomorrow. Having any guy by my side would prevent Anthony from filling the space.

He slides his hands into the pockets of his chinos, a stance that accentuates his nicely rounded biceps, clearly visible because he's still wearing the damn t-shirt.

"I'm sorry for drawing you that way." I spit the words out quickly because humble pie tastes like shit.

"No apology necessary, you did a great job."

"I gave you a huge head." Not oversized, like a typical caricature. The cartooned head spans the width of his chest, making the body I drew look like a twig. A twig with pockets stuffed and overflowing with cash. "Your drawing didn't match the rest. I shouldn't have let my personal feelings about you affect the wedding-party t-shirts."

"You can give me huge head anytime your personal feelings about me affect you," he says, winking. And...there he is. The egotistical player who inspired my artistic rendering.

I glance at the bar and catch Brittany staring. She smiles and waves, forcing me to be polite and return the gestures. She's waiting for Anthony to come back, but clearly not worried that he won't. Because I couldn't possibly be a threat. There's no way Anthony would choose me over her. Over any of the women he's added to his trophy case.

"How many Hope Harbor women have you had sex with?"

Whatever fraction of decent human exists beneath Anthony's slick exterior triggers a wide-eyed expression. It disappears just as quickly, replaced by his usual cocky grin. "Are you looking to get on the list?"

"Gross. Never." I punctuate my conviction with a gagging noise. "Seeing Brittany waiting for you like a pining puppy made me wonder if there's been an uptick in sexually transmitted diseases around town since you started frequenting the place." Because I am the *worst* version of myself in Anthony's presence, I add, "I hope you spend some of your millions on quality condoms." Then I push past him and head for the exit, before one or both of us does something to make me feel worse.

This weekend can't end soon enough.

chapter two

. . .

anthony

I'M NOT A LIAR. Never have been, even as a kid, when lying would've kept me out of shit. But last night, when Mya asked me how many women in town I've had sex with, I couldn't tell her the truth, either. She'd either think the number was too high—confirming her opinion that I'm a man-whore—or she'd laugh because the number's too low, meaning I'm not as "on my game" as I lead people to believe. It was an unwinnable situation.

So I redirected. And that did not sit well with the saucy brunette.

Physically stopping her a second time would've gotten me slapped. Maybe kneed in the balls. Instead, I followed her out of the building, staying back enough to prevent further pissing her off. Which turned out to be too far back, because she'd put half a block between her and On the Rocks by the time I reached the sidewalk.

I texted her. Offered to give her a lift or walk her home. She didn't reply.

Today's no different. She didn't respond to my offer to bring food or drinks while she and Bailey got ready for the wedding. After our few minutes of legit conversation last night, I'm back to being persona non grata.

I shouldn't care, but I do. And it's not just because she's Bailey and Jensen's close friend. That might've been the truth initially, but it'd be a lie now.

Every polished-for-the-public smile she wore during the ceremony and formal photos today pulled the noose on my heart a little tighter. I've seen her genuine smile, it lights her up so much more than the fakes. She's always pretty, but she's fucking stunning when that light is on. I need to see that light. More than that, I want to be the one who flips that switch.

Dinner for two hundred has been cleared. The speeches are finished, the bar has reopened, and nearly every eye in the place is on the newly married couple, currently swaying on the dance floor during the first dance.

My eyes are on Mya. Her deep-blue dress shows off her full tits, and I have to wipe my mouth to make sure I'm not literally drooling.

Her gaze meets mine as I approach, and the smile from her conversation with Bailey's other bridesmaid fizzles, replaced by a straight line.

"Ladies." I nod and offer my hand. "Mya, I believe the pleasure is all mine for the next dance."

"Fine." She says it with a huff, but the sound changes to something softer when our fingers touch. It's the electricity. The crackle and hum that's always between us.

"Is that why you work so hard to push me away?" I ask once I've got her in my arms on the dance floor. "You're afraid of our physical chemistry?"

She's not short, and the heels she's wearing brings us

nearly eye-to-eye. A position she uses to shoot daggers directly into mine. "I push you away because you're an egotistical ass with more flash than substance."

"But you're not denying the chemistry."

"Oh my God," she says, rolling her eyes so hard it must hurt. "That's all you think about, isn't it? Getting your dick wet."

"Actually, it stays pretty dry due to those quality condoms I spend my millions on." The comeback leaves my mouth before I can stop it, and it lands on target, causing Mya to stiffen. I'm fucking this up. Again. "Four."

"Four?" Her gaze narrows to a suspicious squint. "Am I supposed to know what that means?"

"Only if you spend as much time dwelling on all of our conversations as I do." Like last night, until exhaustion shut down my brain. "I've had sex with four women in the past year. I'm not proud of it."

Her eyes widen, then narrow again. "I bet not. You're down, what, around fifty bangs? A guy like you should be nailing somebody new every week."

A guy like you.

"You're going to glare at me with those gorgeous eyes when I say this, but I could've been with more women. I chose not to be."

"Should I call you Saint Anthony?" Her anger shouldn't turn me on, but my dick likes what it likes, and it fucking loves Mya's scathing sarcasm.

"I'm not proud of 'four' because they didn't satisfy me—and before you come at me, I'm not talking about the actual women, or sexual satisfaction. It means, afterward, I felt like the guy you think I am. I regretted those four times, and that's new for me."

"Wow, look at you, growing a conscience after a lifetime of meaningless sex."

"Not a lifetime," I say, pulling her closer while Frankie Valli croons. "And it's not a conscience I'm growing."

"Oh, I *feel* what you're growing, and no soul-baring confession will convince me to let that trouser snake into my lady garden, if that was your plan."

I laugh, loud and full, shaking my head when she tries to pull away. "We're not done, beautiful."

"You had your dance," she says as the music tapers into another song.

"There's a lot more dance ahead for us, Mya. Fifty years' worth, remember? You said you'd get to know me, give me a chance to show you I'm not an asshole. Let's start tonight."

She clucks her tongue. "You're going to prove you're *not* a tail-chasing dog at a wedding reception loaded with available women ripe for the picking?"

"I'm not looking at anyone but you. I pick you."

"I'm not available," she says, letting her hands fall to her sides. "Not to you."

I release her because I'd be an asshole not to. But watching her march away, all sexy curves and sass, I'm more determined than ever.

Mya thinks I only want to get under her satin dress—hell, under any dress—but she's wrong. I'm not lying to myself, or her, anymore. I want to get under her skin, the way she's under mine.

mya

The newlyweds' limo disappears from view, leaving me alone with Anthony, yet again. Everywhere I turned tonight, he was there. Seemingly inescapable, like my shadow, or a foul odor. Only, he smells great. Too great. It's hard enough trying to ignore his good looks. Having to breathe in whatever expensive cologne he wears too...

I should've stopped drinking after the champagne toast. The open bar—another gift from Anthony—meant cocktails constantly flowed my way, despite not asking for any. I'm blaming the buzzy lightness in my head for looking at Anthony *way* too many times tonight. It's alcohol-induced appreciation. Nothing more. I won't be notch number five on his bedpost. But replay everything he said to me earlier... I'll be doing that all night. Including when I'm alone in my bed later. Well, not entirely alone. I'll have my—

"What's going on in that incredibly beautiful head of yours?"

"Bob." *Shit!* Damn tequila.

Anthony's dark eyebrows knit together. "Who's Bob?"

"Nobody." Thank God it's dark out and I'm wearing gobs of makeup. The last person I want seeing me blush is Anthony.

"You're thinking about Bob with a dreamy look on your face, but he's nobody?"

"Fine, he's my boyfriend. I just don't like to talk about him. Our relationship is very private." *Haha!* Nailed it.

Anthony's ever-present smile fades. "I didn't know you had a boyfriend."

"Why would you? We're not friends. We're not anything." Being bitchy is sobering. Also necessary. He's already too close. I can't let him get closer.

"I apologize for making you uncomfortable," he says, tipping his damn handsome head. "Now or earlier. I'm going to call it a night. Do you need anything before I take off?"

Yes. I need him to look at me the way he did while we were dancing. And I need him to mean it—for more than one night. "No, thank you. I'm fine."

"No lie there, you're the finest woman in the place. Bob's a very lucky man." Sparks race up my arm when he catches my hand and presses a kiss to my folded fingers. "Goodnight, Mya."

My throaty, "Goodnight" is swallowed by the summer night as he walks toward the parking lot, rather than return to the hall, where he could easily pick someone up. Maybe he's not the consummate player I pegged him for. If that's the case, why act the part? More importantly, why do I care? *Shit.*

chapter three

anthony

Aside from a glass of wine with dinner and the champagne for toasts, I didn't drink at the reception. Haven't been much of a drinker since winning the lottery. A clear head's necessary when you suddenly have ten million in the bank and everyone wants a piece of the action. Learned that early on.

Since getting back to my rental, I've knocked back four fingers of whiskey, and I'm working on the next four. The alcohol's smoothing the edges upstairs, but it's not numbing the ripping sensation in my chest. I drain the remaining amber liquid, wincing as its heat burns a path down my throat. Physical discomfort is good. I can deal with that a lot easier than emotional shit.

And it is shit. I finally commit to who I want at last call, and every call—and crack that door open, only to find a fucking boyfriend on the other side. One-hundred percent did not see that coming. Probably because I really am an arrogant asshole.

I'm going to have to stay away from Hope Harbor. Not permanently, my friends are here. And though I have zero expectations where my financial investment is concerned, I love seeing their dreams in action. Jensen's bar. Bailey's bakery. Being part of those things, even in the background, is more satisfying than anything I've got going on in Toronto.

But I have to go back. Now that I've accepted my feelings for Mya are much deeper than attraction, and learned she not only despises me but also has a boyfriend...this isn't a good place to be. I'll check in with Jensen's family tomorrow, then head out. Until then, this bartender is serving up another round.

I'm two fingers deep when my phone lights up. A text from Mya. No fucking idea why this is happening, nor do I need to know. Nothing she says at this point will make a difference.

I toss my phone on the couch, swallow another mouthful of *fuck that shit*, and let my head fall back against the pillow. Eyes closed, I inhale deeply, savoring the fog settling in my brain. Yeah. That'll do.

Until my phone pings its reminder of the unopened message, jolting me from momentary peace. Payback from the universe for all the shallow shit I've done? That's what my sisters would say. *Never* telling them about this Mya situation. I'd be hearing about it until my last breath.

I stretch to retrieve my phone, then open Mya's text.

MYA:

I don't have a boyfriend.

Fuck texting. I hit Call and let it ring until her "Why are you calling?" slides into my ear.

"Why'd you lie?" I ask.

"You answer my question first."

"Because I'm drunk, can't stop thinking about you, and would rather hear your voice than tap tiny buttons and hope you reply."

"Wow, okay, that's—"

"Honesty." I tip my head back for another swig. "Or would you rather I lie to you, too?"

"Drunk honesty doesn't count, and I didn't owe you the truth, so don't be a dick."

I set the tumbler down and scrub my hand over my mouth. I think. Everything's a little numb now, including my lips. "You're right."

"I like the direction this is going in, but can you be more specific? Also, this call may be recorded so I can rub it in your face later."

I grunt a laugh. Not too drunk to be amused by the goddess of snark. "Baby, you can rub everything you've got in my face. This call. Your sarcastic mouth that I can't get enough of. Your sexy tits. Your pussy that I just fucking *know* tastes like heaven. Anytime, woman. Any fucking time."

Silence. That's what I get in return for this round of drunk honesty. Shit.

"I've never experienced you drunk," she says, finally. Softly. "And you must be *very* drunk to have said those things to me."

"You're going to hate me even more now, if that's even possible. Fuck."

"I don't hate you, Anthony."

My dick fattens up on the spot. Even the whisky can't compete with the sound of my name rolling off Mya's tongue. I drop my hand over the growing ridge and stroke over the fabric. "Come over."

"Are you too drunk to take care of yourself? Do you need help?"

"If I say yes, will you come over?"

She laughs—genuinely and warmly—and more blood heads to my cock.

Also, some to my brain. To that conscience she accused me of growing. "I don't need help. But I want you to come over."

"I'm already undressed and in bed."

"Okay, I'll come over to your place."

"Anthony!" She's chastising, but also giggling. Mya is giggling. At me.

Fuck. Yeah.

I push off the couch, close my eyes, check my balance. Not one-hundred percent, but I'm not face-planting either. My cock's still hard, so I can't be *that* drunk. It's about six blocks to Mya's place. That'll help.

I pop a mint into my mouth and head for the door. "I'm going to say something, then I'm going to hang up so you don't have to answer."

"Should I say okay, or is that the thing I'm not supposed to answer?"

"Smart mouth." My laugh seems louder outside, but I don't care if it disturbs the other motel guests. "Never change, beautiful. Never fucking change."

"Now I *know* you're super-drunk, because my sarcastic backtalk usually makes you crazy."

"Damn right, it does. I can't get enough of your saucy mouth. Why do you think I initiate group get-togethers every time I'm in town?"

"So that Bailey has someone to talk to while you're shooting the shit with Jensen."

"Bailey doesn't care if Jensen and I hang out. I drag her

into every plan so I can tell her to call you."

"Why?" Her voice is so soft, I might've missed the question if I didn't have the phone pressed tight to my ear.

"I used to come to town to see my friends. Now I see my friends to see you. You make me crazy in the best fucking ways, Mya."

"Is that the thing I'm not supposed to answer before you hang up?"

"So fucking saucy," I say, chuckling. "No, beautiful, *this* is the thing—I'm walking to your place now. I'll be at your door in about five minutes. I'm going to knock once, and if you don't answer, I'll walk away. But I hope you answer the door."

mya

I nearly jump out of my skin when the knock comes. Five minutes isn't enough to make a decision that could change everything. But I'm making it.

Anthony's eyes meet mine the instant I open the door. They don't stay on my face for long, though. Every inch of my body heats as his gaze travels downward. Yes, I swapped my baggy t-shirt and sleep shorts for the sexiest camisole and panties I own. Lingerie nobody has seen because it puts my ampleness on full display. And here I am, letting it all hang out in front of the hottest man I've ever known.

He exhales while pushing his hand through his dark hair. "You look... Fuck, I was not expecting this."

Oh, God. He didn't come over for sex. And I'm nearly naked. *Shit.* "I warned you that I was already undressed and in bed." I cover as much visible flesh as possible by wrapping myself in a hug. "I only answered the door because we're just starting to get along and—"

He shuts me up with his mouth on mine. His hands thread through my hair, and he backs me up to the nearest wall, kicking my door closed behind him.

Okay, so he *did* come over for sex. And I let him in. I'm doing this. It. Him.

His tongue parts the seam of my lips, then slides along mine. He tastes like mint and booze, but mostly, he tastes exactly how I imagined—like sexy heat. Every pass, every second of deep, sensual kissing ratchets *my* heat higher. That's all he does, just stands there, holding my head, kissing me and kissing me, until I'm so hot I feel as if the skimpy lingerie might burn right off.

If I'm doing this, I'm *doing this*. My hands find his trim waist, then I explore. He's so warm. So hard beneath the white shirt he wore for the wedding. I slide my hands between our bodies and work the buttons open, pushing the fabric aside so I can run my palms over his bare chest.

He abandons my hair to skim his hands downward. Along my neck, my shoulders. Lower, to my boobs. Then to the bottom of my camisole, which he peels up, breaking our kiss to remove the scrap of satin.

It's been a long damn time since a man has seen me naked, and the last time was memorable in a really crappy way, instinctively causing me to cover myself now.

"Don't you dare," he says, circling my wrists and drawing my hands away. "I need to see you. A year of staring at your sexy tits through clothes was a long enough wait."

I'm not ashamed of my size. I'm not. There's beauty in the plus. But I'm topless in front of *Anthony*. Hot-as-fuck, totally head-to-toe gorgeous, always-cocky Anthony, who could have any woman he wants, and has had plenty. I'd bet my last dollar none of them have been my size. Maybe that's why he's hitting on me now—for variety. To add a plus-size notch to his bedpost.

"Mya," he says, gently tipping my chin up. "Look at me."

I didn't realize I'd closed my eyes, but they're squeezed tight. His gray eyes are waiting when I open mine, and they're as warm as his other hand where it's cupping my breast.

"We can stop right now." His voice is as soft as his touch. "You let me in, but you can kick me out too. I'd rather leave tonight than leave you with regrets tomorrow."

"I won't have regrets." I might be lying. I won't know until it's over. I do know I'll regret chickening out. I flatten my palms on his six-pack abs, then slide them up, sparks racing through me when the dusting of chest hair tickles the apexes between my fingers. I push his shirt over his broad shoulders, then follow the material down his toned, muscular arms.

"*Mya.*" His voice is rougher as I move to his pants, opening the clasp and zipper. "Be sure, beautiful. Once your hands are on my dick, I won't be as gentlemanly with my offers."

"Are you warning me off your cock?"

"Fuck no. I'm warning you *on*." He inhales sharply as I push his pants and boxers past his hips, then take his thick cock in my fist. "You have no idea how many times I've imagined this night."

"How many?"

"Don't know. Can't count that high." His chuckle becomes a groan when I drop to my knees and swirl my tongue around his cock. "Last call for the gentleman. He's leaving the building the second you wrap your pretty lips around me."

"That's what I want." Holding his gaze, I press a kiss to his tip, then take him into my mouth. Every long, thick inch of him.

"Fuck, babe." He groans as I hollow my cheeks, sucking him hard. "It's going to kill me not to come down your throat, but I won't. Not this time. Going to fuck your mouth, though. Going to make every part of you mine." His fingers thread into my hair again, then he takes control, guiding my head up and down, up and down.

My nose bumps his abdomen with every deep thrust into my mouth. I slacken my jaw and let him drive, heat pooling between my legs at the sound of his groans, the scent of his skin. I squeeze my thighs together, desperate for pressure. For release.

"Too good, have to stop." He groans, pulling me off his cock as salty-sweet pre-cum hits my tongue. "Remember what I said on the phone?"

"Which part?"

His smile is pure sin as he pulls me to my feet, kicks his pants away, then walks me toward my open bedroom door. "The part where you rub your sexy tits and sweet pussy in my face."

"I remember that part," I whisper. *Oh, I remember.*

He turns us when we reach the bed, sitting on the edge, then sliding my panties down. "So fucking sexy," he says, sucking one nipple into his mouth while teasing his fingers between my closed thighs.

I grab his shoulders, my head falling back as he treats both breasts to hot, wet kisses while rubbing circles over my clit. My thighs are shaking, I'm so close. But he doesn't push me over, no matter how much I arch toward his touch. *"Anthony."*

"Time to rub that sweet pussy in my face."

I shriek as he lifts me, seemingly with ease. "Not like this," I say when he lies back, with me centered over his face.

"Exactly like this." He grips my hips, pulling me down—

so close, his warm breath fans my slick, needy flesh. "Ride my mouth, gorgeous."

My body instinctively bears down at the first press of his tongue. "I don't want to crush you. Not when I'm starting to like you."

His chuckle vibrates against my clit, which he kisses while looking up into my eyes. "You won't, beautiful. You couldn't."

"I'm—not a small woman. Obviously."

"I've been staring at you for a year. Believe me when I tell you that you're perfect, exactly the way you are."

The last of my defenses crumble. He may break my heart tomorrow, but tonight, I believe him. I nod, going willingly when he bands his arms around me and draws me down, until my pussy covers his mouth.

God, his mouth. He sucks me, lavishes me with hot kisses. But his tongue, oh God, his tongue. Better than the best bullet, I couldn't resist if I tried. I rock against it, falling onto my forearms and grinding on his mouth as the tingling, buzzy spiral hits.

His growl ripples through me, pushing me into a second wave of sensation from which there's no escape, because his arms are locked around me as he plunders from beneath. Only when I'm panting and giggling does he surrender control of my body.

"Holy shit, woman," he says when I roll off his face.

"Did I hurt you?"

"Only my dick, because you make me so hard it hurts." He's caging me now, looking down into my eyes with a level of passion I've never experienced.

"Pretty sure I can make it feel better."

He groans when I grab his firm butt and pull him tight to

my body, with his cock nestled between my legs. "Gotta grab a condom before I do something you hate me for."

"I won't hate you if you promise you're safe."

"I am." Holding my gaze, he strokes his thumb over my bottom lip. "I'd never do anything that'd hurt you."

Except break my heart when he moves on. But that'll be my fault for opening it.

"Then, fuck me, just like this," I say, running my hands up his broad back and sliding my fingers through his hair. "I want you inside me."

He seals his mouth over mine, sweeping his tongue into my mouth while filling my pussy with one deep stroke. He breaks the kiss, pulling back to look into my eyes when I suck in a breath. "Too much?"

"No, God no. Don't stop."

"Couldn't if my life depended on it," he says, searing me with another kiss. Another thrust. Then another and another. Over and over, each stroke deep and purposeful, hitting my G-spot until I'm writhing beneath him, desperate to go over. "So fucking sexy. Need you to come all over my dick."

And I do, grabbing his ass and pulling him so deep, I can barely breathe as I shatter into a million brilliant pieces.

"Fuck, Mya, *fuuuck*..." His body jerks atop mine, his groan filling my head as he comes while buried deep inside me. "Better let you breathe," he says, nuzzling my neck before rolling to his side. "Even though you took mine away every time I looked at you tonight."

My heart skips in my chest as he wraps his arms around me and pulls me into a spooning snuggle. It might be the alcohol talking. An overflow of romance from watching our madly in-love best friends get married. I should know better than to fall for Anthony. Right now, in this moment, I'm helpless to do anything else.

"You never told me why you lied about having a boyfriend," he says, pressing a kiss to my nape. "Or who the hell Bob is."

"Don't be jealous. You were way better than Bob."

He hugs me tighter, growling against my neck. "Now I'm going to have to kick his ass for ever touching you."

"That'll be hard to do since Bob doesn't have an ass." I've giggled more in the past hour than I have in a year, but I can't help doing it again. "Bob is my vibrator. B.O.B. Battery-operated boyfriend."

"That dreamy look in your eyes was because you were thinking about your vibrator?"

"Partially. I was thinking about going home to use it while pretending it was you." I may never live that admission down, but in his arms like this, I don't even care.

"No more pretending." He slides one hand between my legs and circles my clit, lighting me up with his touch. "I'm here to put Bob out of a job."

"Again?" I ask, my breath hitching as he shifts to notch his cock at my entrance.

"Once was never going to be enough, beautiful."

chapter four

. . .

mya

THE SMILE I forced for my customers withers and dies the moment they exit my store. They gushed about my artwork and spent over three-hundred dollars on a bag full of screen-printed t-shirts and postcards. I should be giddy, but I can't call up an ounce. I feel a lot of things today, but joy and pride aren't among them.

Embarrassment has held the top spot since I woke up alone. No handsome Italian spooning me. No note on the pillow, text or voicemail messages on my phone. I might've wondered if I dreamed the whole thing, except... I don't sleep naked. And I was very naked when I woke up. Naked body, naked heart.

Stupid heart. I could live with the embarrassment of Anthony seeing my naked body—every inch of me, up close and extremely personal. People make reckless decisions when alcohol is involved. If I'd kept my heart locked down and simply enjoyed the sex, everything would be fine today. Better than fine, because the sex was *amazing*. But, no, I believed the soulful look in his eyes. The convincing flattery that left his mouth.

It's fine, I'll get over it. I've been stupid enough to fall for the wrong guy before. I bounced back then, and I'll do the same now. Not immediately, but soon, or...eventually. I won't have to see him for two weeks while Bailey and Jensen are on their honeymoon. That'll help the recovery process. Once my best friend is back home, I'll tell her what happened, and make sure she doesn't include me in any more Anthony-related events.

I don't need to go to Jensen's bar when Anthony's in town. No group dinners or hanging out. I should be able to avoid him completely for almost a year. By the time we're forced to be face-to-face for Bailey and Jensen's baby's christening, I doubt either of us will remember last night.

Who am I kidding—I'm sure Anthony will forget it long before next year. But me? No. As if I could ever forget the hottest night of my life.

The door chime rings while I'm in the back getting product. I flip my internal switch to customer-service mode, gather a breath, and enter the store, my fake smile becoming a grimace when I see who I'm greeting.

"Why are you here?" I'm back to being a bitch. My natural state with Anthony. Last night was a fluke. The sooner I accept that, truly accept it, the better off I'll be. I move to the racks that require restocking. Go about my business as if his presence means nothing. I need it to mean nothing.

"Bad day?" he asks, looping his arms around me from behind. "Bet I can make it better."

My body throws away the get-over-Anthony memo and responds instinctively, pressing my ass against him. "I thought you went home," I say, freeing myself from his hold.

"I went back to the hotel room while you were asleep. I didn't want you to feel pressured when you woke up."

"You didn't want me to feel pressured." I snort and shake my head. "To what? Make you breakfast? I'm quite capable of saying no, and after everything we did last night, it's pretty obvious I don't require pressuring to do other things."

"Not pressure for breakfast or sex."

"I call bullshit." I want to walk away, but my feet won't obey. I want to look away, but my eyes refuse to budge from his handsome face. It's survival instinct kicking in—forcing me to be strong, not vulnerable.

"Why are you so pissed off?"

"I'm not. I'm just going back to the way things were."

"Is that what you want?" he asks, his eyebrows drawing together. "Because it's not what I want."

"I'm not sure what you want, but I know what you *don't* want, and that's to make a big deal out of last night. My empty bed and silent phone told me that much."

"I explained why I left."

"The pressure thing, right. Let's share some sober honesty. You woke up, freaked out about what you did with me, then left," I say, busying myself with hanging t-shirts. "It's fine. I opened my door knowing you'd been drinking. We fucked—a lot, and it was great, you really know how use your God-given tools—but now it's daylight and everything's different. I don't need you coming into my store six hours after sneaking out of my house, pretending we're more than a one-night stand out of guilt or obligation because of our mutual friends. I know what we are and what we aren't. Who you are, and who I'm not."

He holds my gaze for so long, I almost forget why we're staring at each other.

I swallow the ball of emotions that forms when he turns

and walks toward the door. Another minute and he'll be gone. "What are you doing?" I hurl the words at him as he turns the deadbolt and flips the Open sign to Closed. "It's Sunday afternoon in July, my busiest time of year. I didn't win ten million dollars. I need every customer who wants to walk through that door."

"That's really who you think I am? Just a cocky asshole who got supremely lucky in a lottery pool, a guy with nothing to offer except his bank balance and a good-time ride on his dick?"

I wince at his description. That's exactly who I thought he was. Who I needed to believe he was, so I wouldn't like him too much. So I wouldn't fall in love with him.

His jaw clenches hard as he advances on me, but his eyes are warm, swirling with everything *more* I know he is. "I was a starving student, slinging drinks to pay my bills for a program I wasn't sure I belonged in when I won ten million dollars. You know what happens after you hit it big like that?"

"Freedom?"

He grunts. "Financially, yes. But you lose the freedom to make relationships. Everybody's suddenly your friend. Women love you. Only they aren't, and they don't. People love the excitement of endless money, or they're out to get their hands on a piece of the action. I learned that the hard way, Mya. Not just with friends who weren't friends. With a woman I believed loved me. Spoiler alert, she didn't. I don't regret winning the money, because I get to do a lot of great stuff for people I care about. But not being able to trust people, being cynical about everyone new who comes along... It changes you. Not for the better."

"I'm sorry," I say, touching his face. "I never thought about it that way."

"I know. That's part of why I was drawn to you—because

you weren't impressed by my money. You didn't try getting close to me. Hell, you couldn't stand to be near me. The more time went by, the more I inserted myself into your world, the more you seemed to want me out of it. Now that's freedom," he says with a laugh.

I can't stay angry at him, not after hearing all that. But the truth is so obvious. To me, anyway. "I think you liked the challenge I presented."

"Maybe," he says, breaking my heart a little more.

"It's understandable." I step back, wrapping myself in a protective self-hug. "I know that a person's word doesn't mean much after what you've experienced, but I promise I'd never try to take advantage of your financial status. I'm not interested in your money."

"I know you don't give a shit about my money. What about my heart, Mya? Are you interested in that?" He moves into my space, peels my hands from my arms and draws them to our sides, where he weaves our fingers together. "Because it's yours if you want it. I didn't think I'd take it out of the vault for anyone, but I can't keep it locked up around you."

"What are you saying?" I whisper.

"I'm saying I'm crazy about you. I think about you constantly. Every day, I rack my brain, coming up with ways to get close to you, figuring out how to unlock *your* vault the way you obliterated mine."

"You did a pretty good job picking the lock last night." Heat ripples through me when he smiles. When he laughs, freely and deeply. I want so badly to throw myself into that fire, to let it—him, us—consume me. But... "Then you were gone this morning. Without a word. What was I supposed to think, aside from you regretted being with me?"

"That's impossible. What man could possibly regret that?"

"I could name a couple," I say quietly.

"Forget their names, or let me love you so fucking completely, you say their names with a smile on your face, because they were part of the road that brought us here."

Love. He said love. But it's just a word. It doesn't mean he's *in love* with me.

"If that's how you feel, why did you sneak out?"

"I left this morning because I didn't want to pressure you by telling you everything I want with you. You've been pushing me away for a year. A couple of days ago, I wasn't sure you'd ever even like me. I didn't want to scare you away by saying I love you too soon."

Oh. My. God. He said it. There's no holding back my smile. I don't even want to try. I just want to hear him say it again. "There's nowhere else I want to be, and I don't scare that easily, so...try me."

He lets go of my hands, cups my face in his palms, and looks into my eyes so deeply, my knees nearly buckle. "I love you, Mya. I love your sass, your sarcastic backtalk, your creative soul, your incredible talent and gutsy determination. I love your loyalty, your spirit, and your sexy-as-fuck body. I love everything about you. I don't care if we're rich or poor. I'll donate my money tomorrow if you want me to. I don't care where we live, because the only geography that matters to me is your heart. I just want to take you to bed every night and wake up with you every morning. Starting tonight."

"You love me." I blink at him as I process the most romantic words I never expected to hear.

"This is the part where you say it back," he says, winking. "Or you tell me to fuck off. Whichever fits your feelings for me."

"Those are my options? There's no in between?" I ask, digging up some of that sass he apparently loves.

"Not with us, beautiful. There's too much fire between us. We're all or nothing."

"We're all," I say, plastering myself to his chest with my arms around his neck, my fingers in his soft, dark hair. "I love you too. I promise to take care of your heart for as long as I have it."

"How do you feel about forever?"

"It's a start," I say, mimicking his words from the bar two nights ago, when I agreed to *try* liking him.

The sound of the store's door rattling snaps me from my fairytale bubble.

"I better let you get back to it." He kisses me softly, smiling as he walks backward, toward the door. "I'll be back at closing time."

"And then what?" I ask, unable to contain the smile spreading across my face.

"Then we work on moving the needle toward forever."

Possibly the best plans I've ever had.

epilogue

. . .

anthony

A BAR MIGHT SEEM like a strange place to hold a christening party, but it makes sense when the baby's parents own the place. Plus, it's a private party on a Sunday afternoon. It still took some convincing to make it happen, but that's one of my fortes. Sweetening the pot by paying for the party didn't hurt either.

I enjoy hanging out at On the Rocks, but Mya is the main reason I pushed to have the party here. It's kind of *our* place. We met here, we've verbally sparred here more times than I can count, and I'm confident she'd agree we fell in love here —even though neither of us knew it or wanted it at the time. It's the perfect place for what comes next, but I didn't want to be surrounded by strangers. Setting up for this afternoon's party gives us a reason to be here alone.

She's standing on a table, taping streamers to a light fixture when I look up from behind the bar. She's so beautiful, so fucking sexy. And she's mine. Forget the lottery—winning her heart was the luckiest day of my life.

"You look sexy as fuck up there," I say, folding my fingers over the ring in my palm as I walk to the table. "Will you dance for me if I put on music and wave cash?"

Her laughter echoes in the large, empty room. And her smile—god damn, her smile. Prettiest sight in the world. "Put your money away, honey. I'll dance for you later, for free."

I fucking love it when she calls me honey. It started six months ago, after we moved from her apartment to our new house. Things were already great, but something about settling into a place of our own took things to a new level of amazing. More relaxed. Natural. And yeah, even sexier, though I wouldn't have thought that possible. She's always proving me wrong. I love that too.

"Help me down?" she asks. "I shouldn't have climbed up here with my heels on. The table's kind of tippy."

Hello, opportunity.

"With pleasure, beautiful," I say, steadying the chair she used as a stepstool while offering my other hand.

She smiles as I guide her from the table, her eyes going wide once her feet are on solid ground, along with one of my knees. "Anthony?"

I'll never get tired of hearing my name on her lips. Still holding her hand, I look into her gorgeous dark eyes and hold up the ring. "I had a speech lined up, but now all I can think of is to tell you I love you and can't imagine my life without you. Marry me, Mya. Promise me I get to love and cherish you for the rest of my life."

"That's not really a question," she says, her luscious lips curving into a saucy smile.

"You're right." I slide the ring onto her finger, then tug her onto my knee, and kiss her until I'm hard as steel and she's breathing my name against my lips. This is our dance. We push and pull, but we always come together. She's my queen, there's nothing I wouldn't do for her, including do this the way she deserves.

"What're you doing?" she says as I lift her from my knee and wiggle the ring off her finger.

"Getting it right." I hold up the ring again. "Will you make me the luckiest man in the world and be my wife?"

"Yes. God, yes." She waggles her fingers, squealing when I slide the ring on again. Then her arms are around my neck, her fingers are in my hair, and her lips are on mine.

And my heart is wide open and locked up tight at the same time. In the vault with only one key—her love.

Thank you for reading Last Call Casanova! I hope you loved Anthony and Mya's story as much as I do. There are more books in the Hope Harbor series! Find them all on my website:

www.karladoyle.com/books/hope-harbor-series

IF YOU HAVEN'T READ Jensen and Bailey's friends-to-lovers romance yet, you can get **Dad Bod Wingman** in ebook, paperback, or audiobook!

Join my mailing list to stay up to date on all the news!
www.karladoyle.com/newsletter

Visit **www.karladoyle.com** to view Karla's complete library.

also by karla doyle

Just in Queso (Man of the Month: Magnolia Point)

Gift Wrapped

Cup of Sugar (Close to Home—Book 1)

Icing on the Cake (Close to Home—Book 2)

Sweet as Candy (Close to Home—Book 3)

Body of Work (Very Personal Training—Book 1)

Worth the Wait (Very Personal Training—Book 2)

Game Plan

More Than Words

Crossing the Line

Visit Karla's website for the most up-to-date list:

www.karladoyle.com

hope harbor series

Hope Harbor is a fictional small town on the north shore of Lake Erie, in Ontario, Canada. There are other real-life cities and towns mentioned in the Hope Harbor books. With a little geographic investigation, you might be able to pinpoint Hope Harbor's location on a map.

All books in the Hope Harbor series are standalone stories focused on a different couple's romance. You'll visit the same settings across multiple books, and there may be some character crossover pop-ins, but there's no reading order. Start anywhere in the series, and follow whatever path you choose in Hope Harbor! They all lead to a satisfying happily ever after.

Hope Harbor Series

Dad Bod Wingman
Heart Beats
Last Call Casanova
Fleshing It Out
The Deal With Love
Doggy Style
King of Her Dreams
Her Pipe Dream
12 Days

These books are linked to the Hope Harbor Series, but take place in a different location:

Resorting to Love
White Lie Christmas
Heart of Texas

Check Karla's website for the most up-to-date list of Hope Harbor Series books.
www.karladoyle.com

An Excerpt from
DAD BOD WINGMAN

**When a buddy hits on the woman
Jensen has secretly loved since childhood,
his days of being "the wingman" are over.**

I've always been the wingman. The great buddy. The teddy-bear guy women lean on.

In elementary school, I was the kid passing notes between infatuated classmates. In high school, I was the guy telling a pretty girl that somebody liked her. In college, I was the icebreaker, initiating casual conversation with women in the bar, so that my buddies could ultimately take them home.

Tonight's no different, even though it's my birthday. I'm still the guy enlisted to lay the groundwork so my friend can get laid.

Only tonight is different. Because tonight, we're in my hometown. In my bar. And tonight, the woman I've been asked to warm up is Bailey Burrows. That's not happening.

Yeah, I owe my buddy. The guy invested in my business when the bank laughed in my face. But I'm still not helping him hook up with the girl I've crushed on my entire life. If anybody's taking Bailey home, it's going to be me.

CHAPTER ONE

jensen

The bank said our town couldn't support another bar. I told the bean counters they underestimated the spongy quality of our livers here in Hope Harbor. It'd earned me a laugh, but hadn't netted a business loan.

Looking around at the steady flow of customers on my third Saturday night in business, I'm glad I didn't take the bank's "no" as a final answer. And I'm thankful as hell I accepted my buddy's insistence on backing the place.

Anthony had laughed off the investment with an easy, "I'll catch you for a favor sometime." Thank fuck he's just a lucky bastard who won the lottery a few years back, not part of the mafia.

My never-silent partner has been here since the doors opened tonight, cruising the room with a tray of complimentary shots. "On the house," he says, or, "Cheers to the birthday boy, Jensen." Stuff like that. He never takes credit—just pays with it. All those *free* shots are courtesy of Anthony's platinum card. There's a heart of gold under the superficial party-boy image he projects.

By ten thirty, On the Rocks is packed wall-to-wall with bodies. My marketing manager made sure all of Hope Harbor knew tonight would be my big, dirty-thirty birthday party. Not my idea, but it worked.

I swear, nearly everyone I've met between birth and high-school graduation has walked through the door tonight. Everybody has a smile and a story from back in the day. It's awesome. A relief, too. Hope Harborites can be fickle about new businesses started by out-of-towners. I was away for twelve years, but apparently, I still count as one of the locals. It's good to be back.

Anthony joins me at the bar, sliding another tray of empty shot glasses across the polished wood top. "When you brought me along for the walk-through of this abandoned craphole, I wasn't sure it could live up to your dreams—and it didn't."

Well, fuck. "Don't hold back, Anthony. Tell me what you really think."

"That's what I'm doing, dumbass." He punches my shoulder—a pointless action, since I've got nearly a hundred pounds on him—then motions for the nearest bartender to fill the tray with a round of fresh drinks. "The place looks amazing, man. The finished product blows your concept ideas out of the fucking lake." He nudges me, winking and nodding. "See what I did there? Lake, not park."

"Good one." I acknowledge the latest in his never-ending string of lake-related puns, then add, "And thanks. The compliment means a lot, coming from you."

"Because I'm a shit-talking asshole?" He grins while handing his credit card to the bartender.

"Because you were the second-best wannabe architect at university."

"Look who's the shit-talking asshole now," he says, liberating two shots from the newly filled tray. He puts one in my hand and raises his glass for a toast. "To your new baby. Now, time to get rid of this one." And because he *is* a shit-talking asshole, he jabs my stomach, where it's testing the endurance of my shirt's two lowest-visible buttons.

"Yeah, yeah." I lean over the bar and dump my shot in the sink. Not because I give a shit about the calories. I don't. Haven't for a long time. I just want to be one-hundred-percent clearheaded while I'm on the job, that's all.

"Hey." Anthony backhands my arm as I'm wiping the bar. "Please tell me the hot blonde who just walked in is part of the 'everyone loves Jensen Rockford' club, because I want an introduction. That pretty little fishy is definitely putting her sweet lips on my hook tonight."

I know who his latest lake pun is about before I turn around. *My* favorite hot blonde. Hell, my favorite woman of any description. Bailey Burrows. I've had one eye on the door all night, waiting for her to show up, like she promised when I ran into her at the coffee shop this morning. Or yesterday, when I literally bumped into her with my shopping cart at the corner of canned goods and crackers in the grocery store. Because everywhere I go since moving back to town, Bailey is there. Yeah, being back in Hope Harbor isn't so bad at all.

"A-fucking-plus," Anthony says, when Bailey spots me and waves as if we haven't seen each other in years. "It's good to know a guy who can hook you up."

My head whips in Anthony's direction fast enough to hear my neck crack. "What?"

"The blonde. Hook me up, bro."

"No." I shake my head because, fuck that shit.

"Why not?" He laughs as if I just told some hilarious joke. "This is our dance, dude. You're the wingman. You reel them in with your nice-guy schtick, then I throw them back after giving them *my* big stick."

"Not this time."

"Why not? Because the whole town will come after me with their fishing poles if I break her heart?"

"Not the whole town," I say, gritting my teeth hard enough to hear the friction echoing in my ears.

The lights go on behind Anthony's dark eyes. He slaps his hand on his leg and howls. "You like her."

"Of course I like her. We've been friends since kindergarten."

"That's it?" he asks, and I nod. "Then I'm calling in my favor. Introduce me to blondie, hang around 'til she settles in, then leave her to me."

"She's not your type." The bar squeaks in protest beneath the unnecessary scrubbing I give it. "She's a nice girl." That ought to do it. I've been Anthony's wingman more times than I can count since we met at university. He's a good friend, but lazy. With all things in life, including women. He goes for the sure thing.

Anthony's attention shifts to Bailey as she works her way through the crowd. He whistles under his breath as she bounces toward us, all smiles and sunshine—and tits. "Favor time, man. Let's see if I can fuck the 'nice girl' right out of your cute little friend."

Bailey reaches us before I have time to react—aka, punch Anthony in the face. But when he checks her out like a hungry man at an all-you-can-eat buffet, I'm tempted to throw the fucking punch anyway.

"Happy Birthday!" she squeals, throwing her arms around my neck and pressing all her incredible soft parts against me.

I swallow her tiny frame inside an oversize bearhug. It'd be rude not to, she's been a friend since forever. And, yeah, I'll take any excuse to be this close to her. Especially with Anthony ogling her ass as if he owns it.

She releases me from the mega-hug, flattens her palms on my chest and stretches to place a kiss on my cheek. "Thirty looks good on you."

"Thanks. Your turn in a couple weeks."

"Oh, my God, how do you remember my birthday?"

"You know our buddy, Jensen," Anthony says, butting in.

"He's probably got everyone's birthday on a master calendar, so he doesn't forget to send a Facebook message."

Bailey blinks a couple times, then laughs. "That is possible." She smiles up at me while issuing a playful poke. At least this one's in my chest. "I do see your handsome avatar on all kinds of happy-birthday posts. That's a great picture of you, by the way."

I'm not completely lacking in confidence, but hearing Bailey call me handsome is an unexpected win.

Anthony takes my momentary silence as an opportunity to wedge himself between us. "Jensen here may have the best Facebook manners, but he's falling down on the in-person job. I'm Anthony. And you're the most gorgeous woman in here."

Bailey's gaze shoots past Anthony, to my face. The bar is semi-dark, but I swear there's a question in her eyes.

No matter what I do, somebody's going to lose. I don't expect to come out the winner—that's not how it works when you're the wingman—but I'm sure as hell not letting Bailey be the loser. Hopefully she'll see him for the player he is. One way or another, she's not going home with him.

I exhale, doing my best not to scowl. "Bailey, this is Anthony Marini, a good friend of mine from Toronto. We started out in the architecture program together, then Anthony won the lottery, literally, and dropped out of school."

Her eyes open wide enough to show the whites around her brown irises. "You actually won the lottery?"

"Yup. Ten million." He loves telling this story. Fucking loves it. Probably because it almost always leads to getting laid. "I was waiting tables seven nights a week to make tuition and rent, and one of the other waiters asked me if I wanted to join their lottery pool. I handed over ten bucks I couldn't afford, and boom, next day, we were splitting one of those mega-jackpots."

"Wow, that's amazing," she says. Typical response.

This is the part where I'm supposed to smooth the way for Anthony. Make the woman feel at ease with him, so he can flash his smile, and string the girl along, right into his bed.

Not happening tonight. "Anthony's your man if you're looking for a fun one-night stand with a guy who'll buy all your drinks. If you'd rather be with someone who'll take their time, stick around, and treat you the way you deserve, long-term, you should resist the moves he's about to put on you."

Anthony's head jerks back and Bailey's bottom lip drops. There's about five seconds of everybody staring and nobody speaking.

Then a belly laugh rips from Anthony's mouth. "Holy shit, man. I didn't think you had it in you."

I know where he's headed with that comment, but it's not happening. One of a wingman's skills is subtly redirecting, and that's what I plan to do. "Wingman shoots down the pilot —it's treason, I know. But Bailey's been a friend longer than you have, so she gets priority."

There's a glint in Anthony's eyes. He's brewing up trouble in that bored brain of his.

All I can do is hold my breath and hope he chooses to be less of a dick than me.

"All right, you get a pass—for now." He points a finger at me. "Don't waste it, it's a limited-time offer."

Nope, not responding to that one. Which is an acknowledgment in itself.

Anthony's grin tells me he knows it, too. "I'm going to lubricate the crowd," he says, picking up the tray of shots. Because he *is* a good guy, just one who can't keep his dick in his pants. He tips his head at Bailey. "Nice to meet you. And I spoke the truth when I said you're the most attractive woman in here."

"It was nice to meet you, too."

I snort at her blatant disregard of his obvious, last-ditch attempt to pick her up. The sound doesn't go unnoticed—by either of them. Fuck. I need to get a handle on the jealousy I have no right feeling.

Bailey's attention shifts from me to Anthony. "Sometime when you're not busy, I'd love to hear stories about Jensen in his college days."

Anthony grins. "You got it, gorgeous."

"There are no stories about me," I say, after my buddy has disappeared into the crowd, the loaded tray perched on one hand, skilled waiter that he is. "I started in architecture, switched to business, worked my ass off, and graduated. That's about it."

Her hair shimmers as she shakes her head. "I don't believe you."

My fingers twitch at my sides. I've wanted to touch that blonde silk since puberty. Because I'm a sucker for self-torment, I chose to sit behind her in class every chance I got. Teachers accused me of daydreaming a lot back then, and they were absolutely right. They'd be up front, talking about whatever subject it was, and I'd be watching Bailey's hair dance on the edge of my desk.

"A hot guy like you, on a campus full of hormone-fueled twentysomethings? Please. Even if you weren't a party boy like your friend, I'm sure you had all the women you wanted, and broke lots of hearts."

First handsome, now hot. If I didn't know better, I'd think Bailey was flirting with me. But I do know better. She's being nice, because she's a nice girl. Always has been.

"Can I get you something?" I ask, moving behind the bar. "On the house."

"That's not how you stay in business." Her bubbly laugh is as pretty as everything else about her. "Didn't they teach you anything in those fancy courses of yours?"

Thank fuck I'm supposed to be focused on her right now, because I couldn't look away if I tried. "I'll put it on Anthony's tab, how about that?"

"Sounds reasonable. I'm pretty sure he wanted to buy me a drink."

"Yeah, well, this is as close as he's going to get." I manage to contain the growl, but not the grimace that goes with it.

"Why, Jensen Rockford, are you being possessive, or is this a brotherly, protective thing?"

I grunt a laugh. "Not brotherly."

"In that case, I approve."

I know she's just being playful, so I smile and shake my head. I'm the trustworthy teddy bear. The guy women turn to when they need a safe male presence. They play with me, then put me back. That's how it's always been.

"What's your drink of choice?" I ask, gesturing at the bottles and taps around me. "I bartended my way through college, I can probably make whatever fancy thing you like. I even have little umbrellas, and those swords for spearing cherries."

She leans on the bar, effectively putting her cleavage on display, front and center. "If only you'd offered to put your sword in my cherry before leaving Hope Harbor."

There's nothing in my mouth, but I choke anyway. Audibly. Loud enough that my actual bartender pauses what he'd been doing to look over at me. I motion for him to carry on, and try to unscramble my brain while Bailey smiles at me. I'm a pretty chill guy, but I don't have a clue how to respond to her comment. Because there's no way she meant it seriously. Not a chance in hell.

"You're cute when you're flustered."

And now I'm *cute*. Something's up tonight, and I think it's Bailey's blood-alcohol level. I tip my chin and shoot her a smile. "I think somebody did a bit of pre-drinking before heading over here."

"I had a few glasses of wine with Mya." Pink rises to her sun-kissed cheeks. "But I'm not drunk."

"Just priming, I get it." I also get that's why she's being extra flirty. "Still hanging out with Cheryl, too, like you did back in the day?"

She nods. "You have a good memory. Cheryl stayed in town after high school, same as me. Mya left for college, but moved back a couple years later."

"Nice."

"I've been lucky," she says, holding my gaze. "All my favorite people either stayed in the Harbor, or have finally moved back."

That *finally* refers to me. I'm not a cocky guy, but I feel the intent of that single word all the way to my core. And lower, because my cock *is* a bastard. If I serve her another drink, she'll probably say more things that'll sound too good to be true. But I'm a glutton for more than just carbs, so I make the offer.

"Have you decided what you want?" I ask, bracing my arms against the bar top.

She nods again.

"All right. What'll it be?" Thank fuck for the cover of the bar, because my cock really likes watching her pull her full, bottom lip between her teeth. "Rethinking your decision?"

Her wavy hair shines under the bar lights as she shakes

her head. "I know what I want, I'm just nervous about saying it."

"This from the girl who just joked about me spearing her cherry," I say, giving her a wink. "What do you want—sex on the beach, a screaming orgasm, a creamy pussy?" My smile practically stretches ear-to-ear when her face turns red. "Don't be embarrassed to tell me. I've heard it all."

"I bet you have." She sighs and eases back from the bar, robbing me of—or saving me from—the previous primo view of her cleavage. "I'll just have a beer. Something pale, whatever you have on tap."

"Are you sure? Because I'll give you anything. Happily." If she knew the full depth behind my words, she'd probably run out of the bar and never look back. Good thing she thinks I'm talking about her drink choice.

She gives me the pause signal while pulling her phone from her back pocket, swiping the screen and holding it to her ear. "Hey, I'm at Jensen's bar. What's up?"

I wait, watching her face shift through a variety of expressions. Listening to her make a series of evasive noises. My stomach drops when she issues me a scrunched-up nose while silently mouthing, *I'm sorry.*

The call only lasts a few more seconds, then she slides the phone back into her pocket. "That was Cheryl. She's having a moment and needs to talk."

Fuck. "Yeah, of course. Give her my best."

"I will."

"Thanks for coming by tonight," I say, moving out from behind the bar. "It's always great to see you."

"You too." She throws her arms around me for another hug that smashes her soft little body against mine. "Happy birthday, Jensen."

I nod as she releases me. Safer than opening my mouth,

because when she's this close, it's hard to stay where I belong —in the friend zone. I give the standard buddy wave as she walks away, then another one when she reaches the door and looks back at me.

It's probably not great that she caught me staring, but whatever. If she remembers me watching her leave, she'll probably remember the flirty things she said, too. I doubt she'll want to bring those up anytime soon.

"Bro." Anthony appears at my side, seemingly out of nowhere. "That girl was at the head of the line with a basketful of premium product, credit card in hand, and you failed to ring up the sale." Everything's a metaphor with Anthony. To be fair, he's got a knack for them. "And don't try saying you're not interested in hitting that, because I've never seen you look so dopey around a chick. *Or* act like a possessive caveman." He gives me a thumbs-up and nods. "That was your one good move of the night, by the way. Blondie dug it, too. It was obvious."

"Nice try," are the words that exit my mouth, because there's no way I'm fueling Anthony's master-of-all-things-woman complex. But, fuck. What if he's right?

"Holy shit," he says, slapping my shoulder. "Do not go to Vegas with that face, man, because it will spit you out faster than a virgin with a mouthful of jizz."

"You're a pig."

"That's true. I'm also right. I knew you were interested in blondie the minute you cut me down. But you're not just looking to hit that fine ass, you're in love with her."

I grunt at him, hoping it's more effective than my other attempts to throw him off the scent.

It's not.

"The only way she could've made her interest clearer would've been sticking her tongue in your mouth. Which she'd probably be doing right now, if you hadn't fucked it up so badly," he says, stepping behind the bar and helping himself to a bottle of beer. "This one's on you, by the way. Call it a stupidity tax."

"Fuck that. Take it off what I owe you."

"See?" Beer in hand, Anthony points at me. "That's the guy who should've stayed out to play. You've got to take yourself off the bench, dude. Put yourself in the game."

"Not with Bailey."

"Give me one good reason why not," he says, raising the bottle to his mouth. "Aside from you're a pussy."

I snag the beer before his grinning face makes contact, tip my head back and drain the whole damn bottle. "She admitted she'd been drinking before she came in here. I've known her a long time. She wouldn't have said those things if she wasn't under the influence."

Anthony tips the hat he's not wearing. He's a grade-A player, but he's not a douche. "That leaves me with one question."

"How can you be as classy as me?"

His full-blown laughter draws the attention of everyone on the south side of the bar. "Not even remotely interested in that." He nabs another beer from the fridge and whips out his credit card, raising his eyebrows when I motion for him to put it away. "There he is, the good-guy-next-door your cute little schoolyard friend fell for. And I don't blame her. But you've got to call up some of that take-charge shit. Combine it, bro. Then track down the hot blonde while she's sober, and take her fine ass on a date. No asking. *Tell her* you're taking her out. Not as friends. On a fucking *date*. One that includes fucking."

I cross my arms over my chest and button my lips.

"Your poker face hasn't improved in the last ten minutes,

man." He laughs because he knows he's right. Fucker. "Look. I do a lot of questionable things with my life, but have I ever tried fucking with yours?"

"No."

"Then think about it. Yes, she's been drinking. But she wasn't wasted drunk, not even close. She was loose-lips tipsy, at most. Meaning, she said things she's probably wanted to say while sober."

Fuck, I hate it when he has a good point.

"No need to thank me, the lightbulb going on above your head is thanks enough."

Anthony laughs at my scowl and takes a long swig of beer. "Enjoy the rest of your birthday by listening to the cash registers sing. Go home, pull up Bailey's Facebook profile—because I know you've got it favorited—and spank the monkey good and hard to her picture."

"You're such a pig."

"Yeah, and you know you're going to do it." He laughs while ducking my jab. "Then, tomorrow, when she's sober and you're not walking around with Mount Dickmore in your pants, you track her down, and tell her it's on."

I track her down, and tell her it's on. Sure. Sounds simple enough...now. Tomorrow's another story.

Dad Bod Wingman is available now in ebook and paperback!

An Excerpt from
HEART BEATS

**Pulling a fan onstage during the concert
is just part of the show, until the jaded rock star
meets the muse he wasn't looking for...**

jagger

The media calls me "Jaded Jagger" and they're not wrong. I wasn't just a rising star, I was the rock industry's sunshine from the moment I debuted, and that instant mega-stardom put me on center stage, 24/7. Money, fame, women... Anything I want is mine for the taking, and I've taken plenty. It's all disposable. Things stop mattering when you have the world at your feet. When all you have to do is show up, and whatever you want is automatically yours.

That's how I assume it'll be when I pull a gorgeous brunette onstage during a concert. It's part of the gig. The crowd loves it, and the female fans I choose are always very grateful after the show. They don't call it a backstage pass for nothing.

Only... something's different tonight. Every cell in my being lights up the instant I take the brunette's hand. When I sing my chart-topping rock ballad to her, the words have meaning. She's different. Special. Important. I don't know how, but I know. There's a connection. I don't just want to bury myself in Maria's hot body, I want to lose myself in her.

When the music ends, she disappears into the crowd instead

of going backstage. But our song isn't over. I didn't believe in muses—or love at first sight—until this woman. Now that I've found her, I'm not letting her get away.

CHAPTER ONE

jagger

Another city. Another stadium. Another packed house. I've lost count of how many times we've played in Toronto since I started touring sixteen years ago. Many.

Every city, every audience, likes to believe it's the best of the bunch. A belief we fuel by telling each one they're our favorite. A white lie that's good for the energy and for business.

We've finished the first three songs of our set when the band tapers off instead of leading into another. Time for me to spin the harmless lie. Hype the audience even higher than they already are, and that's pretty damn high. Hard to imagine they can scream any louder, but we're going to find out.

"It's been too long, Toronto! I love being back here in the T-dot."

The house erupts in a raucous roar. Mic in my hand, I raise my arms, encouraging them to make more noise as I walk back and forth across the front of the stage. Lighting makes it impossible to see faces beyond the first few rows, but I smile out at the crowd as if I'm making eye contact with every single one of them.

The fans I *can* see are primarily female. We're a rock band with a massive male following, yet the first two rows are packed primarily with women, many of them smokin' hot. That's how it always is. Not complaining—I like the view. Especially the brunette at center stage. I always pull a fan onstage during the show, and tonight, she's the one. I knew the instant I saw her.

The volume of the crowd doesn't decrease when I lower my arms. They're supercharged, this audience. The euphoria of playing to a sold-out audience faded a long time ago, but I still appreciate the fans' enthusiasm, so I tuck the microphone under my arm and give *them* a round of applause, along with a wolf-whistle. They fucking love it, and I find myself honestly enjoying the moment.

"You guys want to know a secret?" I ask, bringing the mic to my mouth.

The response is a thunderous, screamed *"yes"* that makes me laugh.

"All right, here's the secret—every city we're in, we tell them it's the best. But right here, right now," I say, pointing at the stage, then around the packed stadium. "There's something extra about this place, about the people. I really gotta move here someday, because Toronto rocks!"

The crowd loses its fucking mind. I've played some wild shows to crazed audiences, but the volume in the stadium right now has to be a record.

I turn and point at the band. Johnny lays down a beat on the drums. That's all it takes for the fans to recognize our current number-one single. Shane, Luke, and James follow on keyboard and guitars. By the time I belt out the first line, the place is practically vibrating, and I feel more alive than I have since we started this tour six weeks ago. Longer, even. Maybe the euphoria's not completely dead.

There's no break after the last verse. We transition seamlessly into the next song, another recent chart topper.

Belting out the lyrics, I cover every inch of the stage, moving back and forth, again and again. Doesn't matter what my mood is, or how I feel, I fucking perform. That's what the people pay to see, and that's what they get. Every time.

I'm rocking the house, but I can't stop looking at the gorgeous brunette. She's not waving a sign or jumping up and down. She's not wearing skimpy clothes or gobs of makeup. There's nothing excessive about her. But there's *something* about her.

I point at Shane as he takes center stage for a guitar solo to finish the song, then I duck out of sight to change my shirt and scrub a towel over my sweaty face. Have to look the part when I'm pouring my heart out in the rock ballad coming up.

"Going to slow things down for a few minutes," I say, returning to the stage. "Give this old guy a chance to rest. I'm not as young as I used to be."

There's laughter and roaring from the crowd. Voices calling out that I'm not old. They're right, I'm only thirty-three. But I've been hardcore touring since I was seventeen.

Once the buzzing from the crowd subsides, I bring the mic to my grinning mouth again. "How do y'all feel about *Tomorrow*?"

Applause and hooting fill the air. The song isn't everyone's cuppa, but it sat on the Billboard chart long enough to know it's a crowd-pleaser for most, especially the female fans.

"All right," I say, crossing the stage. "I'm going to need help with this one." My white dress shirt a sharp contrast to the snug-fitting black t-shirt I started with, and anyone who's been to a show before knows what happens next. Most of the women in the front row know, that's for damn sure. It's tits-bouncing, arms-flailing central down there.

There's no question in my mind, no contest. My gaze locks

on one woman as I move toward the edge of the stage—one of the few *not* trying to get my attention.

Her eyes open wide when I crouch and extend my arm. She looks left and right, then points at herself when I give her the come-hither motion.

"Yes, you," I say, as one of the stage crew pushes a step block in place against the stage. "Want to come up and join me for a song?" The mic picks up every word, and fifty thousand people scream their approval.

As does the dark-haired woman standing beside her. "Hell yes, she does!" she yells, giving a hearty but affectionate shove to my brunette's shoulders. "Go, girl. Go!"

My beauty steps forward, taking my hand along with the first stair. The instant she touches me, a jolt rips through me.

"Sorry, I think I gave you a shock," she says, attempting to break free of my hold.

I don't let go, tightening my grip instead. Not for the show. Not for practicality. That wasn't static electricity passing between us. A physical reaction, yes. Something more than that, too. I can't tell her that, though. Not with the equivalent of a small city watching every move, listening to every word. Damn, what I wouldn't give to be alone with her.

Later. After the show. I'll take her somewhere. Not to my dressing room for temporary satisfaction. Somewhere where we can truly be alone, where I can take my time.

The crew has moved the grand piano into place on center stage, and that's where I lead her. I squeeze her hand before releasing it, motion her onto the glossy black bench, then take my place beside her.

I smile at her while playing a few bars of a song nobody's heard before, including me, because it didn't exist until this minute. "What's your name?"

"Maria." Her brown eyes open wider as the microphone

mounted on the piano broadcasts her voice to the crowd. "I didn't expect it to pick me up," she says, then she laughs. Light and effortless, but also a bit husky. The sexiest laugh I've ever heard.

I shift in place, making room for my expanding cock. Been a long time since I reacted to a woman this fast. Forever since I got hard just being near someone. My dick has become pretty jaded over the years, just like the rest of me.

"Maria's a pretty name." Yeah, I say that to every woman I bring up for the ballad. Sometimes I mean it, sometimes I don't. It's the God's honest truth in this moment. "Are you from Toronto?"

She shakes her head, making her dark hair sway. "Hope Harbor."

"Haven't heard of it," I say. "Is it nearby?"

"About ninety minutes southwest. My sister dragged me to the show."

I stop playing long enough to cup my hands over my heart as if I'm wounded. "Not a fan?"

"I am. I like your music. Just not cities, crowds, and craziness in general." Another sexy laugh leaves her full, rosy lips. "I'm just a boring, small-town girl."

Still playing the new music she's brought to life inside me, I turn my face toward the audience and lock eyes with the woman who must be her sister, the one who pushed her to come onstage. "Is that the truth? Is Maria a boring, small-town girl?"

"She's lying to you, Jagger! Maria's not boring at all," the woman calls, snapping her fingers above her head. "Ask her if she likes to sing!"

"On it..." I lift one hand long enough to point at the woman bearing a strong resemblance to Maria, yet whose appearance does nothing for me. "What's your name?"

"Mya! If you're ever in Hope Harbor, make sure you stop by my t-shirt shop, Mya's Art In Fact, and I'll hook you up with some excellent stuff!"

"Y'all hear that?" I point out at the tens of thousands of other fans. "Road trip to Hope Harbor tomorrow, so we can buy every t-shirt in Mya's store. Deal?"

The crowd roars, and my gut-deep laughter booms through the sound system. "All right, I better see a lineup down—" I look to Mya again and ask, "What street's your shop on?"

"Main Street!" Mya jumps up and down, shaking her curvy form as if she's a game-show contestant who just won a prize. If even a small percentage of tonight's audience shows up tomorrow, she's definitely going to win.

Pretty sure I can make that happen, and maybe catch a win for myself in the process. "Make some noise if you're going to meet me at Mya's t-shirt shop tomorrow at two o'clock."

The audience sounds like thunder. My manager's going to sound the same way when he finds out I've just scheduled myself for a public appearance that'll fuck with our travel plan. That's tomorrow's argument. As for tonight, I've completely derailed the show and I don't give a fuck. Beside me, Maria is laughing, and I know right now I'll do anything to hear more of that perfect sound.

I abandon the audience to face her, awareness rocketing through me when our gazes meet and lock. "Do you like to sing, Maria?"

"When I'm alone. I sound great in the shower."

"I bet you do." I smile widely, hoping the comment comes across generically instead of pervy. Because it's definitely pervy in my head. The thought of water rolling down her naked body while I fuck all kinds of great sounds from her has my cock straining like a battering ram against my fly. "No shower here and you're not alone, but you're welcome to sing along."

I switch to the tune I'm supposed to be playing, my bandmates following me into *Tomorrow* as my fingers move over the ivory keys. The notes and words come as automatically as breathing. The song is exactly the same as the thousands of times I've performed it, but each line that leaves my mouth feels different. I wrote this love song for nobody. Singing it while looking into Maria's eyes, I feel like I wrote it for her. I just didn't know it at the time.

Her gorgeous eyes don't leave mine for a second. She smiles through the first verse, but her lips remain closed in a beautiful smile. Until I reach the chorus. Then she sings. Only one line, but it's fucking magical. The tiniest tease of her siren's voice. That's all she gives me, but it's enough to make me feel as we're alone in this moment of minutes, instead of the focus of fifty thousand people.

By the time the song ends, she's leaning in, her body turned toward me, her shoulder pressed to mine. Her eyes have the glassy sheen of barely restrained emotion, and it takes everything in me not to cup her face and claim her parted, rosy lips.

I've kissed women onstage before, but it's always calculated. A cue to my crew to make sure the woman is waiting for me backstage at the end of the show.

My need for Maria is different. She's not someone I'll fuck and forget by the next show. I don't know how I know—I just do.

Instead of marking her as my pick of the night, I take her hand and bring it to my mouth. Soft and gentle isn't my thing. I don't have time to woo a woman or take it slow. Everything in my world moves fast, then moves on. Only, I don't want to use her and lose her. I want to know her. Really know her.

No idea how I can realistically make that happen, but it doesn't start with me banging her in my dressing room.

Luke must be a mind reader, because he moves to the front of the stage and launches into a guitar solo to cleanse any rocker's palette of the heartfelt ballad I just performed, buying me time to escort Maria offstage.

I rise from the bench while holding her hand, every cell of my being wide-a-fucking-wake as we walk into the wings. The handheld mic is on the piano. We don't exactly have privacy, but it's as close as we're going to get for now.

"I'm glad your sister dragged you here tonight."

"Me too. Your natural voice is fantastic. It's refreshing, because that's not the case with all live performances, especially from artists produced by major labels."

"Thanks," I say, chuckling. Compliments from female fans are normal, but never like that one. I've got seconds left with Maria. Not nearly enough. "I've gotta get back out there, but you're welcome to watch the rest of the show from here. We can talk more after the encore."

A wave of applause signaling the end of Luke's solo steals my ability to hear Maria's answer. Now I've really got to get out there. Shrugging an apology, I release her soft hand, then trot my ass back to work. Behind me, the band goes all-in on *Sugarcoated*, a gritty pulse-pounder. It drops as a single next week, and if all goes according to plans and predictions, it'll be another number one.

I don't take time to introduce the song, I just dive in, belting the lyrics as I crisscross the stage, working up a fresh sweat that turns my white shirt nearly see-through. It's intentional. Everything about the show is—except those unscripted minutes with Maria.

Minutes that are over, and I don't have time to think about because the show must go on. There's not even an opportunity for me to look for her in the wings.

A couple of songs later, I spot her in the front row. Seconds later, she and her sister disappear into the depths of the stadium... and don't come back.

The audience doesn't know it's a chore for me to finish the set. That my enthusiasm during the encore is fake. I'm a performer. An actor. I've given the world exactly what they wanted and expected for the last sixteen years.

Even my bandmates can't tell my head's not in the game. They're used to me withdrawing to my dressing room after a show. Nobody'll knock because everyone expects me to be getting my freak on behind the closed door. That's what goes down. Has since my first tour. How many seventeen-year-olds lose their virginity to not one, but three gorgeous women, all enthusiastic about doing anything and everything? Not damn many, I'm sure. Thank God I've tamed the fuck down since then.

A stealthy escape and brief cab ride later, I'm at the hotel, with none of my bandmates or tour crew the wiser.

"Good evening, Mr. Marsh," the concierge says as I enter the lobby from a side entrance. "You're the first to arrive for your group's afterparty, but everything is ready to go in the executive suite."

"The afterparty. Shit." I exhale while raking my fingers through my hair. "How about you never saw me come in?"

"Of course, sir." The man doesn't miss a beat or show a hint of emotion. "If there's anything you'd like delivered to your suite with the utmost discretion, since nobody has seen you arrive, simply call or text that number," he says, handing me a business card.

"Thanks. I'll do that." I nod, then head for the service elevator. By the time I reach my floor, I've requested a platter of light finger foods, three large bottles of sparkling water, and a bucket of ice to be delivered on the sly. My buddies can do all the partying tonight. I've got a song to write.

maria

The city where I put my foot in my mouth disappears from the rearview mirror as the highway stretches as far as my eyes can see in the darkness.

Mya snorts when I tip my head back and groan for what has to be the hundredth time since we left the concert. "Are you going to torture yourself all the way home?"

"Yes." I'm definitely replaying my dufus comment in an infinite loop for the next ninety minutes. Then all night, tomorrow, and probably for the rest of August.

"Here, this'll help." Mya taps some buttons on her car's stereo display, bursting into laughter when her choice in music makes me groan again.

"How is listening to *that song* going to help me?"

"Oh, it's not. But it's sure helping me!" She swats my hand when I reach for the controls. "No way, chica. Listening to Jagger pour his sexy heart out—*again*—is your penance for botching a once-in-a-lifetime chance to bang a rock star."

"You're a mean sister."

Mya lets the faux insult roll off. She knows I don't mean it. She's also laid-back in ways I never will be. In ways I can't even pretend to be.

"Why can't I be normal?" I ask, sighing. It's a question I've asked more times than I can count in my lifetime, though it has been a while since the last time.

"You're *Maria* normal, and there's nothing wrong with that."

"Until I unleash the full effect of *my* normal on a rock star. I can't believe I said that stuff to him. Jagger Marsh chose *me* to go onstage. He held my hand, privately thanked me coming to the show, and my response was to tell him he can actually sing, and that it's refreshing since lots of famous musicians can't? Who says that to a world-famous, mega successful musician?"

"Only you," she says, snorting another laugh. "Only you."

I slap my hand across my eyes and groan. "Where was my brain?"

"In your pants would be my guess. Or in Jagger's pants. Did you see the bulge he was sporting? Holy shit, he must be packing an anaconda." She takes her eyes off the road to shoot me a hubba-hubba expression. "You could be taming that trouser beast right now if you hadn't insisted on leaving."

"No," I say, dropping my hands onto my lap. "He politely offered me to watch the rest of the concert from behind the curtain and said we could 'talk more' after the show. That's not a man who wanted me to *tame his trouser beast*."

"Oh, sweetie, did you not see the way he looked at you while singing that song? Or before and after it, for that matter?"

"It's an act, Mya. I was a prop."

Focused on the road, Mya shakes her head. "Nope. I disagree. He was into you."

"Want to bet on it?" I retrieve my phone from the depths of my purse, and type *Jagger Marsh pulls a fan onstage during a concert* in a Google search. A page of video links populates my screen, which I wave at my sister, even though she can't look closely enough to see the proof. "See? I win." And lose, as the tiny sliver of hope I might've been wrong withers and dies.

"Well... to hell with Jagger Marsh." Mya glances over long enough to locate my hand, from which she plucks the phone, then tosses it into the backseat. "His anaconda's probably poisonous and his show was a snore."

"Anacondas aren't venomous, and he's an amazing performer."

Mya sighs, shaking her head when her pun flies over my head, as so many do.

A knack for humor isn't one of my gifts. I *might* be able to tell a joke if my life depended on it, but I hope it never comes to that.

"Aside from super-dorking yourself out of a backstage pass with the sexiest rock star of our generation, did you enjoy the concert?"

"I did. You would've had a better time if Bailey could've gone instead, but thank you for talking me into it."

"You mean guilt-tripping you into it, but whatever. I have no shame." She snorts, then glances over. "And stop about Bailey. She's my best friend, yes, but I had a great time with you. We should do more stuff together now that I've moved back to Hope Harbor."

"I like that idea."

"Me too," she says, smiling at me. "Tonight was fun. Plus, if you hadn't taken Bailey's ticket at the last minute, I wouldn't have gotten that awesome free publicity for my store. Thank *you* for being gorgeous and irresistible—even if you are a dork when you talk to rock stars who want to bang you." She laughs when I respond with a hard poke to her shoulder, nearly veering into the other lane when she returns the gesture with competitive sibling gusto.

I sigh as our shared laughter tapers into comfortable silence. Having different personalities and lifestyles hasn't prevented us from becoming close, even if it took a while to get here.

"Do you think Jagger will actually show up at your store tomorrow afternoon?"

"Nah," she says, flapping a hand. "He was working the audience. And maybe trying to impress you. He probably won't even remember saying it. But the diehard fans will, and I bet some show up. Maybe lots." She shrugs. "Anything's possible."

One thing that's not just possible, it's definite—that at two o'clock tomorrow, I won't be anywhere near Mya's store. I've had all the crowds and excitement I can handle. Plus, the sooner I put tonight's dorktastic encounter with a rock star in my personal rearview mirror, the better.

Heart Beats is available now in ebook and paperback!

about the author

A small-town girl with some big-city experience, Karla resides in Southwestern Ontario with her husband and two young-adult children. She studied fashion design in college and spent 20+ years working in that industry before succumbing to the writing muse. When she's not writing the sexy stories that swirl around in her head, you can find her playing online Scrabble, or cuddled up with a book and her adorable pets.

Karla loves hearing from readers! Connect with her online, or send her an email: karla@karladoyle.com.

Visit Karla's website to see all her books:
www.karladoyle.com

Join Karla's mailing list to stay up to date on all her news:
www.karladoyle.com/newsletter